Mac
the
Sock

PAGE PUBLISHING
Conneaut Lake, PA

First originally published by Page Publishing 2022

ISBN 978-1-6624-5841-5 (pbk)
ISBN 978-1-6624-5842-2 (digital)

Printed in the United States of America

Mac the Sock

Welcome to Sock World

JOSEFINA A. GENAO

It was a Saturday afternoon, and mom was cleaning the house. Mom asked Megan and Joseph to help her with the laundry and put the clothes away before they went out to play. They were folding clothes and becoming upset when they noticed that the other half of some of the socks were missing.

Mom walked into the room to check up on them and noticed them frowning.

Mom asked, "What's wrong? Why have you stopped?"

"Mom, we're trying to match these socks and these two are missing their pair," Joseph explained.

Mom laughed and said, "That's okay, that's normal. They just went off to Sock World."

"Sock World?!" yelled Megan and Joseph together.

"Okay," mom said, "sit and let me tell you a story."

"When socks are washed, they go through cycles in the washing machine. A magical window opens and when it opens, one or two lucky socks will enter. I'm not sure how a sock is picked, but it is drawn to the window and goes into Sock World."

Hearing this made Megan and Joseph curious. They stopped what they were doing and asked their mom to tell them more.

Mom laughed and began to tell them a story of a little girl named Kristy and her favorite pair of socks. One was blue and the other was red. They were big and comfortable.

She loved them so much that she named her socks Mac and Julie. She handwashed them separately and hung them to dry. She was careful, as she didn't want to cause them too much wear and tear. She didn't just use them on her feet, she used them as hand puppets and blankets for her dolls.

One day, Kristy's mom was cleaning and went into her room and picked up the socks. She put them in the washing machine. While they were in the wash, bright lights appeared, and a magical window opened and pulled Mac in.

Mac the Sock found himself in this new world, feeling a little confused and scared.

Everything was different. Everything was colorful and bright. He looked down and noticed he had legs, so he began walking. As he walked around, he bumped into a pretty pink sock that was long and thin named Demi.

Demi looked over at Mac and said, "Hi, you look confused, you must be new here!"

"Yes," Mac replied in a low, shy voice.

Demi smiled and said, "Welcome to Sock World!"

"Come on, I'll show you around. You'll love this world!" Demi said.

As they walked, they passed a bright-yellow sock with polka dots and athlete socks that were surrounded by other socks that were pink, red, orange, and green. There were all kinds of socks that you could imagine.

As they walked past a field, they noticed socks with team numbers playing soccer. On the sides of the field, there were colorful socks with pom-poms cheering.

DANCE

They came across a plaza. There was a dance studio and several offices. He saw solid-colored socks with briefcases, doctor's lab coats, and socks with business suits.

They stopped in front of a daycare, and peeked inside. They saw baby socks sleeping, while others were being read to.

Mac asked Demi if all the socks arrived the same way he did. Demi said, "Yes, you can stay here forever if you want." Mac was happy when he heard her say this, but then started thinking about Julie and how much he would miss her.

It was getting late, so Demi said "Come let's go to my house, you're welcome to stay with me."

They walked up to a bright yellow house. "Welcome home," exclaimed Demi.

Demi prepared a room for Mac. "Sleep well, tomorrow will be a big day" whispered Demi. Mac laid down and smiled, excited for his new adventure to come.

About the Author

Josie has always had a passion for helping and supporting those in need. She has worked with FEMA providing housing resource information for natural disaster victims. Josie has also worked as a Guardian ad Litem, where her dedicated advocacy ensured a child's safety, well being, best interests, and permanent home placement. In her spare time Josie makes an effort to volunteer at church for fundraising events, charity work, and a variety of community outreach programs.

Josie is married and has five children who are adults now. When her children were young they helped her with the laundry as one of their chores. They frequently had to ask her what happened to all of their socks, because some would always seem to disappear. Since then, those socks have been missing. And, now we all know, they are in Sock World.